# Captain Vlad

## and the
# Mary Rose

### Kate and Sam Cunningham

It's a huge task, but we have always risen to the challenge.
Thirty-four years ago my great, great, great, great, great
grandfather watched young Henry VIII launch the Mary Rose.
In the many battles since then we've captured sixty French
ships and caught scores of Scottish pirates.

There are always unexpected hazards. Even at the start
of this voyage we had to face a new danger.

It all started just after collecting our food
and equipment. We supervised the loading.
Nothing seemed unusual.

Everyone settled in.

I gathered the new crew to give them a rousing speech.

'Welcome, rats. There may be some rough weather in the next few days, but there's plenty to eat and I'm expecting a quiet journey.'

Beg pardon, Captain, but what are you planning to do about the dog?

PLUCKE

We set out to search.

Teams of rats explored every nook and cranny. We searched between cannon balls and coils of rope; we looked under bedding rolls and in sacks of shoes.

There was no sign of the enemy.

However, as we reached the gun deck, the smell hit us.

It was true.

There was a dog aboard the Mary Rose.

We scurried along the gloomy deck, until we were outside
the carpenter's cabin.

The stench was overpowering and fear made my legs shake.
This closed door was all that separated us from terrible peril.

We could only imagine the hideous beast
prowling around and gnashing his teeth.

Roxton shuddered as we rushed past to
find the other creature. Surely there
couldn't be a hawk on board too?

Up and up we went, until we came out onto the open deck and
into the bright daylight. There were fewer places to hide here.
Roxton scampered forwards towards the castle deck,
but we soon found what we were looking for.

The dark shadow of the hawk slid across us as it flew overhead, and suddenly it didn't feel so warm outside.

We'd seen enough, so headed back down to the safety of the hold.

Overnight the wind got stronger, and the sea churned and thrashed as if it was alive. The ship was tossed around on crashing waves, throwing us up in the air and then dropping us.

The smell in the hold became unbearable. It was damp, it was dark, and it seemed the night would never end.

The hull of the ship creaked, and Sludge the carpenter was busy filling every tiny gap with hair and tar to stop water getting in.

Finally, it was dawn and the storm had passed, but there was
no chance to rest. It was time to carry out the plan.

Every rat knew what they had to do, and was
in position. On my signal we were off.

Plucke darted past the oven, scooping up a juicy piece
of meat - the bait we needed to tempt the dog.

He threw it up to Fyshe who was tucked inside the
pouch of the cabin boy's belt.

As they reached the storage deck, Fyshe
dropped the meat into the paws of the
waiting twins, Gripe and Tripe, who were
hiding in the box of short arrows.

They caught it just in time as the archers arrived to carry the box up to the gun deck, with the twins stowed away inside.

When the archers put the box down, the twins shot out.

Tripe and Gripe raced along the deck,
zig-zagging between feet and shot,
until they reached the carpenter's cabin.
Tripe threw the meat and now we had
Hatch the dog's attention.

I was tucked behind the door with Roxton, and now it was our turn to carry out the final stage of the plan.

I gripped on, as Roxton jumped out and caught the meat. He bolted towards the end of the deck with the dog close behind.

Roxton grabbed hold of a rope just as Grimbolde gnawed through the last strand holding it down. The rope flew up, yanking us onto the upper deck.

High above us the hawk was in the sky stretching her wings and having her morning exercise. Immediately she spotted our movement, and her sharp eyes widened at the thought of having us for breakfast. She swooped down with her claws out to catch us, just as Hatch burst onto the deck and sprang forward too.

At the last possible moment Roxton dived for a rope,
swung over the rail, and escaped the clash of talons
and teeth as the dog and hawk collided.

Roxton landed niftily on a cannon below, and rolled
back in through the open gunport to safety.

We could hear the angry shouts of Captain Carew who was furious that his hawk had been attacked.

The plan had been a huge success. Hatch, the dog was locked in his cabin for the rest of the voyage. He could no longer frighten the hawk ... or us.

Since then our journey has been much calmer.

As we head to Portsmouth I wonder what the future will be?

## 1 week later ...

Once the Mary Rose arrived in Portsmouth, King Henry VIII watched her go into battle with 80 other ships. They were defending England against over 200 French ships, carrying up to 30,000 men.

Henry had been king for 36 years and the Mary Rose had been the first ship he built when he was just a teenager. He had spent years creating a Royal Navy, and this was its biggest test.

The English ships were outnumbered, but the French were defeated and fled.

However, on the 19th July 1545, during the Battle of the Solent, the Mary Rose sank.

Henry had lost his favourite ship.

Less than two years later Henry would also be gone. He died in 1547 and left his nine-year-old son, Edward VI to be king. The Mary Rose had sailed through most of Henry VIII's reign. When she sank, she became a time capsule of things that ordinary Tudor people used in their everyday lives.

Turn the page to see what happened next to the Mary Rose.

# 435 years later ...

In the following years divers recovered
thousands of objects, before she was raised
to the surface again in 1982.

Can you find the objects
in this picture, and then
in the story?